MISSION ALERT

ALERT

LAB 101

First published in 2017 by Bloomsbury Education
copyright © Benjamin Hulme-Cross 2017
Illustrations copyright © Kanako & Yuzuru 2017
Kanako & Yuzuru are represented by Good Illustration Ltd

Darby Creek
A division of Lerner Publishing Group, Inc.
241 First Avenue North
Minneapolis, MN 55401 USA

For reading levels and more information, look up this title at
www.lernerbooks.com.

Main body text set in ITC Goudy Sans Std 14/24.
Typeface provided by Monotype Typography.

Library of Congress Cataloging-in-Publication Data

Names: Hulme-Cross, Benjamin, author. | Damerum, Kanako,
illustrator. | Takasaki, Yuzuru, illustrator.
Title: Lab 101 / Benjamin Hulme-Cross ; illustrated by Kanako and Yuzuru.
Other titles: Lab one-oh-one
Description: Minneapolis, MN : Darby Creek, [2018] | Series: Mission alert | "First published
in 2017 by Bloomsbury Education." | Summary: "Tom and Zilla are regular boarding school
students—except when they're working as special agents for the government. Their next
mission is to uncover a sinister secret project at a robotics center"—Provided by publisher.
Identifiers: LCCN 2018007210 (print) | LCCN 2018014492 (ebook) | ISBN 9781541525917
(eb pdf) | ISBN 9781541525818 (lb : alk. paper) | ISBN 9781541526341 (pb :
alk. paper) | ISBN 9781472929655 (ePub) | ISBN 9781472929662 (ePDF)
Subjects: | CYAC: Spies—Fiction. | Brothers and sisters—
Fiction. | Twins—Fiction. | Robotics—Fiction.
Classification: LCC PZ7.1.H86 (ebook) | LCC PZ7.1.H86 Lab 2018 (print) | DDC [Fic]—dc23

LC record available at https://lccn.loc.gov/2018007210

Manufactured in the United States of America
1-44565-35496-4/4/2018

MISSION ALERT
LAB 101

BENJAMIN HULME-CROSS

Illustrated by
Kanako and Yuzuru

MINNEAPOLIS

Tom and his twin sister Zilla go to a boarding school. They don't like it very much. But Tom and Zilla have a secret. They work as spies for the Secret Service. Sometimes there is a spy mission that children are better at than grown-ups. That's when Tom and Zilla get their next Mission Alert!

CONTENTS

Chapter One

Tom and Zilla sat at their computers. Their homework was coding, and Tom was working hard.

"You're so slow at coding," laughed Zilla.
Tom didn't answer. He wanted to finish
the line of code he was writing. Then,
suddenly, the screen went blank and they
both groaned.

Sometimes the school computers shut down without warning. It was very annoying!

Then their watches started buzzing, and a message flashed on each of their watch screens. MISSION ALERT!

Zilla and Tom plugged earbuds into their watches. The watches had lots of special spy features. The Secret Service could find Zilla and Tom at any time by tracking their watches. They tapped the screens, and the instructions began.

"Agents, here is your next mission," they heard Marcus say. Marcus was their handler at Mission Control. "It will take place as part of a school trip."

Tom and Zilla looked at each other. They didn't think it would be easy to keep their mission secret if they were surrounded by people who knew them. Missions that took them away from school were much better!

"As you know, you'll be taking a field trip to a robotics center this week," said Marcus.

This was true. Everyone in their grade at school was excited about the trip. Someone had said that remote control robot battles were held at the center.

"We set up this whole trip just to get you two inside the robotics center," said Marcus. "The center is owned by a company that has links with dangerous criminal gangs. Last month one of our spies hacked into the robotics center's systems and found plans to build a huge number of robots. We think they are planning to hire them out to the gangs."

"Why would the criminal gangs want to rent robots?" asked Zilla.

"That's what we want you to find out," said Marcus. "The emails talked about Lab 101, which is inside the robotics center. Your mission is to get into Lab 101 and find out what is going on."

"But why can't you just close the place down, or break in and arrest everyone?" Tom asked.

"We've been watching the center for weeks now, and the only people who go in or out are groups of children on school trips," said Marcus. "We haven't seen any adults enter or leave the building. We need more information before we go in."

Then Marcus showed them some maps and floor plans of the robotics center. He told Tom and Zilla to study the maps so they would know where everything was inside the center and how to find Lab 101.

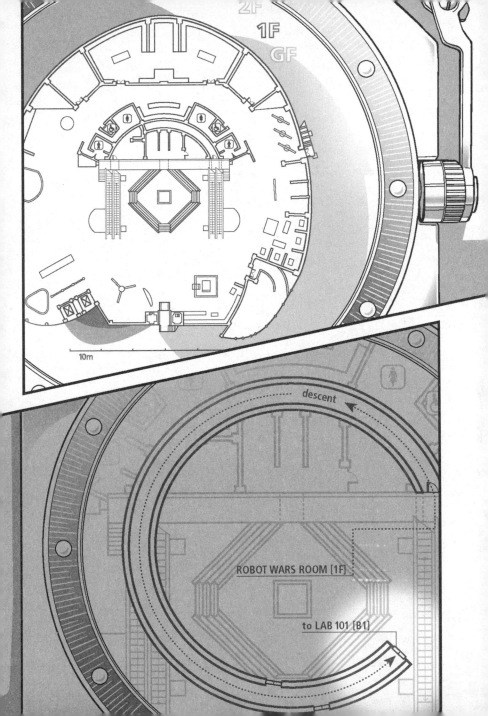

2F

1F

GF

10m

descent

ROBOT WARS ROOM [1F]

to LAB 101 [B1]

Chapter Two

The day of the school trip arrived. All the students were very excited. Their teacher, Mr. Stevens, was not allowed to go into the center. It was just for kids.

So Mr. Stevens stayed in the entrance area. A tour guide dressed in purple led the children over to a short tunnel. *That guide has very bright blue eyes*, thought Zilla.

"To get into the robotics center we have to go through this scanner one at a time," said the guide. "We scan everyone who comes here so that we get better and better at creating robots who can move like humans."

One by one, the students went through the tunnel, standing on a very slow conveyer belt. Zilla was last. When it was her turn, the guide held open the gate and she stepped onto the conveyor belt. On the way through she felt as if she were inside a computer.

She heard a very high-pitched noise all around her. Very bright lights spun around her as she passed through. It felt really strange, and Zilla was glad to get to the other side.

When she got out of the scanner, Zilla saw
a huge sign hanging from the ceiling: ROBOT
WARS ROOM. A group of children was
standing around Tom. Zilla saw that Tom had a
remote control in his hands. He was controlling

a robot that was zooming around in a pit in front of him. A few people dressed like the tour guide were trying to fix the robots that had gotten broken when they crashed into each other. There were bits of metal everywhere.

Tom seemed to be having fun. *I bet he's forgotten why we're here,* thought Zilla.

She looked around the large room they were in. In each corner was a security camera. All four cameras seemed to be pointing at Tom and the other kids. The tour guide was standing near the tunnel they had come through. He was just staring straight ahead with his strange blue eyes.

Over on the other side of the room, Zilla saw more people dressed in purple. She wondered if they had strange eyes too. She walked toward them. Sure enough, they had the same blue eyes that were a bit too bright.

Then one of the people suddenly opened a door and left the room. Zilla saw that he opened the door using an ID card that hung on his belt. It gave her an idea.

She went back to the robot pit in the middle of the room, looking for a sharp bit of metal.

She saw what she needed and picked it up. Then she walked over to the tour guide and stood next to him. Very carefully, she reached out a hand and found his ID card. With the piece of metal, she cut the string, and then she slipped the card in her pocket.

Time to find out what's going on in Lab 101, she thought.

Chapter Three

As soon as the door hissed closed behind her, Zilla felt better. There was something not quite right about the tour guide and his coworkers, and it was good to get away from them.

She remembered the map from Marcus's instructions, and she set off along the white corridors of the robotics center. In less than two minutes she was standing outside a door with a sign that read, Lab 101.

There were no windows into the lab, and Zilla had no idea what she would find inside. She took a deep breath, waved her tour guide's ID card over the scanner next to the doorway, and went in. She left her coat on the floor to stop the door from closing behind her and looked around.

The room was completely white. The only things in the room were three computers lined up on a long table in the middle. She walked across to the computers.

An image of a loading wheel took up
most of the central screen. Under the loading
wheel were the words:

DO NOT ADJUST UNTIL PRINTING
IS COMPLETE.

The screen on the left showed live footage of her friends, still looking down into the robot pit. There were three kids with remote controls now, and three robots crashing into each other on the ground. She couldn't see Tom anywhere.

Maybe he's on his way, Zilla thought, looking at the third screen. This screen showed an image of Zilla herself in the scanning tunnel on the way into the center. The image was a close-up of her face. A grid of bright green lines was shining on her skin in the picture. *Scary,* she thought.

"I'm going to find out what they're printing and then get out of here," Zilla said to herself.

At the back of the room was another door. It had a small window in it. What she saw through the window gave her the biggest shock of her life.

A huge machine was building something. The machine was like a giant arm. It looked like the sort of thing you might find in a car factory. And it seemed to be building a human being.

The human figure that the machine was building wore purple clothes. It was almost complete. The only thing missing was the head. Where the head should have been, Zilla could see lights and wires. Just then, the machine's arm twisted up and over the purple figure, bringing a head down to rest on its shoulders.

It's 3D printing a robot! Zilla thought.

Then Zilla looked at the head. Her heart nearly stopped. Looking back at her, through bright blue eyes, was her own face!

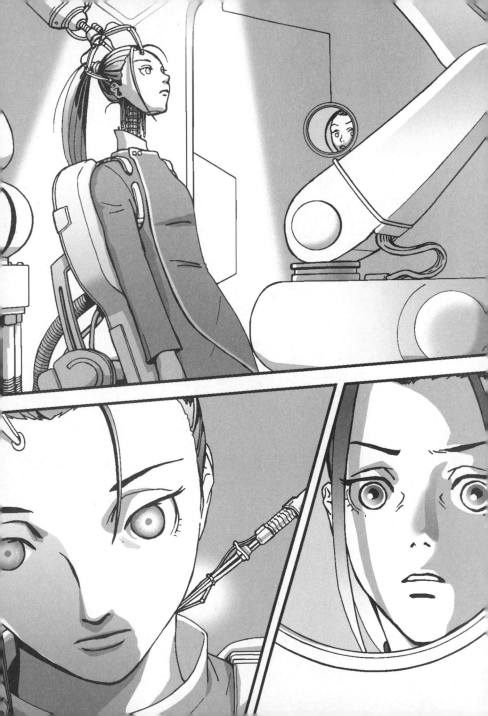

She watched as the robot Zilla was switched on. Robot Zilla looked around the printing room, then turned and left through a door at the back of the room.

"So they're making robot doubles of kids!"
thought Zilla. Her fear was mixed with anger.
She waved the ID pass over the scanner,
walked through the printing room, and
followed Robot Zilla through the final door.

Chapter Four

Just as Zilla walked through the final door,
Tom entered the room with the computers
in it. He had no ID card, but he had followed
one of the people wearing purple out of the
robot wars room.

When he got to Lab 101 he found the door held open by Zilla's coat.

Tom walked over to the computers, just like Zilla had done before him. The middle screen now showed:

EDIT SINGLE ROBOT SETTINGS OR SELECT ALL.

Tom scratched his head and looked at the other screens. One still showed the robot wars room. The other showed line upon line of purple-clothed figures. They were all standing very still, except for one who was walking toward the back of the group.

With a gasp, Tom saw that it was Zilla. At least, he thought it was Zilla. A moment later he saw Zilla following Zilla. There were two of them! One wore purple clothes, and one wore Zilla's normal clothes.

Of course! he realized. *That's why they scanned us! They're making 3D copies to clone us!*

Just as this thought flashed through Tom's mind, he saw that the rest of the purple robots had begun to move. All together, they were walking toward the real Zilla. They had blocked off her path back to the door.

He could see that she was screaming, and he ran to the door of the printing room. But he had no ID card, so he couldn't open it.

He ran back to the computers.

EDIT SINGLE ROBOT SETTINGS OR SELECT ALL.

Tom clicked "SELECT ALL" and hoped that he could find some way of stopping the robots.

He looked at the options:

LANGUAGE SETTINGS

WEAPONS SETTINGS

SLEEP SETTINGS

Next Tom clicked SLEEP SETTINGS.

He looked again at the screen showing Zilla and the robots. They had made a wide circle around her now. She was trying to push her way through them and they were stopping her.

On the screen Tom saw that SLEEP WHEN HUMANS ARE PRESENT was one of the options. Tom selected it and hit ENTER. A loading wheel appeared on the screen.

The circle of robots around Zilla was getting closer and closer to her. She tried to push them away but they were much too strong for her.

Tom noticed their bright blue eyes. It was the clue he needed to work out what was going on. "The whole place is being run by robots!" he gasped. "That's why Marcus said they didn't see any employees entering or leaving the building." On the screen Tom could see Zilla trapped in a circle of robots.

Then the loading wheel on Tom's screen disappeared and, at once, all the robots stopped moving and closed their eyes.

Zilla gave one of the robots a push. It fell over, knocking all the other robots over like a line of dominoes.

Zilla ran to the door, through the printing room, and back into Lab 101. She gave a cry when she saw Tom.

"It's okay," said Tom. "I've put them to sleep."

"Look at this," said Zilla. She had found a folder behind one of the computers. It had lots of pictures of robots with human faces.

"So that's why they scanned us on the way in," said Tom. "Each robot is a copy of a real person. If you're going to break the law you hire one of the robots to do it for you. Then if there are witnesses, the person who the robot was copied from gets the blame instead of you."

"I think we've found out what goes on in Lab 101," said Zilla. "Let's get out of here and report back to Marcus."

Quiz Time

Test your knowledge of the story by trying these multiple choice questions. Look back at the story if you need to. There are answers at the end.

1. What was Tom working on when the Mission Alert came in?

   a. math
   b. history
   c. reading
   d. coding

2. What did Zilla and Tom have to plug into their watches to find out about the mission?

   a. earbuds
   b. mini TV sets
   c. phones
   d. microphones

3. Who arranged the school trip to the robotics center?

   a. the class teacher
   b. the principal
   c. the Secret Service
   d. Lab 101

4. Why did Zilla take a sharp bit of metal from the robot pit?

   a. to harm the guide
   b. to cut the string on the guide's ID card
   c. to open a door
   d. to write a message on glass

5. What did Zilla use to stop the door from closing behind her?

   a. her bag
   b. the metal she had taken
   c. her coat
   d. her shoes

6. What gave Zilla the "biggest shock of her life"?

   a. the size of the building
   b. Tom being held prisoner
   c. all the robots
   d. the 3D printer printing a human

Do you think you would like to be a spy like Tom and Zilla? Write a story about yourself being a spy and solving a case. What gadgets you would use? What villain would you have to defeat?

Answers to Quiz Time

1d, 2a, 3c, 4b, 5c, 6d

MISSION ALERT

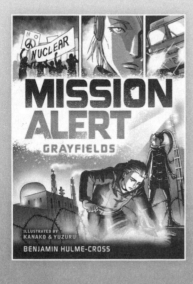

MISSION ALERT

GRAYFIELDS

ILLUSTRATED BY
KANAKO & YUZURU

BENJAMIN HULME-CROSS

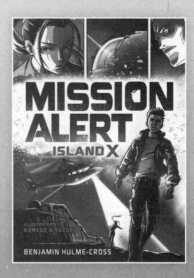

MISSION ALERT

ISLAND X

ILLUSTRATED BY
KANAKO & YUZURU

BENJAMIN HULME-CROSS

Look out for Tom and Zilla's
next spy mission!

CHECK OUT ALL THE TITLES IN THE
MISSION ALERT SERIES

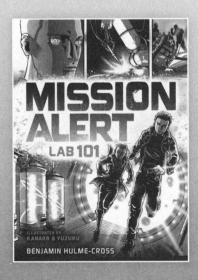

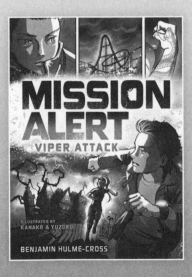

About the Author

Benjamin Hulme-Cross has written over thirty books for emerging young readers. Prior to becoming a full-time writer, he worked for a publishing company, editing novels and plays for high schools. He is currently the director for Iffley Publishing in the United Kingdom.

About the Illustrators

Kanako and Yuzuru are two Japanese sisters who collaborate on every illustration, even though Kanako lives in London and Yuzuru resides in Japan. Using traditional pen and ink, plus a computer, they have done many illustration projects for children's publishing.